Another
Grand
Adventure

 PRESS

Los Angeles · New York

CONTENTS

Copyright © 2020 Disney Enterprises, Inc. All rights reserved. Published by Disney Press, an imprint of Buena Vista Books, Inc. No part of this book may be reproduced or transmitted in any form or by any means, electronic or mechanical, including photocopying, recording, or by any information storage and retrieval system, without written permission from the publisher. For information address Disney Press, 1200 Grand Central Avenue, Glendale, California 91201.

Lost at Sea, First Edition, April 2012
Perry Speaks!, First Edition, June 2012
Attack of the Ferb Snatchers!, First Edition, October 2012
Boogie Down, First Edition, February 2013
First Bind-Up Edition, September 2020
1 3 5 7 9 10 8 6 4 2

ISBN 978-1-368-06575-7
FAC-029261-20199
Library of Congress Control Number: 2020936492
Printed in the United States of America
Visit www.disneybooks.com

SUSTAINABLE FORESTRY INITIATIVE
Certified Sourcing
www.sfiprogram.org
SFI-01415

Lost
at
Sea

Adapted by **Leigh Stephens**

Based on the series created by
Dan Povenmire & Jeff "Swampy" Marsh

One afternoon, Phineas and Ferb went sailing with their parents and their sister, Candace. Their friend Isabella went, too.

Phineas saw flags ahead. He asked Isabella what they meant.

"The blue flag means crab season," she explained. "And the yellow flag means hold the mustard."

The last flag was red with a black square.

"Storm warning!" cried Isabella.

Suddenly, the sky got dark.
"Who turned off the sun?" Candace
asked.

It started to rain. Waves crashed
over the ship, and lightning flashed.

The sailboat was tossed into a large
whirlpool!

When the storm cleared, the boat
had crashed by an island.

"Kids, are you all right?" Phineas
and Ferb's dad asked.

"We're fine," Phineas answered.

But Candace had an
octopus stuck on
her head!

"Mom and I will fix the boat," their dad said. "Candace, why don't you look for food? And, boys, you can find us shelter. We may be here for a while."

"You mean we're stranded?"
Candace asked her mom and dad.
"We'll be stuck here forever eating
rocks and bugs! I'll have to marry a
monkey and have monkey kids!"

Phineas and Ferb weren't worried.
They looked for shelter with
Isabella. Soon they found a patch
of palm trees.

"This has potential," Phineas said.

Phineas drew plans in the sand.

Ferb cut branches.

A snake helped Isabella paint.

Together, they built a tree house!

Meanwhile, back at home, Phineas
and Ferb's pet platypus, Perry, was
in the backyard.

The boys' friends Baljeet and
Buford were watching him while the
family was away.

None of them knew that Perry was a secret agent called Agent P!

Suddenly, Perry got a call on his secret agent wristwatch. His boss, Major Monogram, needed his help.

But Perry couldn't get away without the boys seeing him.

Major Monogram sent Carl the intern to help Perry escape.

Carl pretended to be an ice-cream-truck driver. He headed to Baljeet and Buford.

"Ice cream!" the friends cried.

While Baljeet and Buford ordered,
Perry sneaked into the truck.
He put on his secret agent hat.

"Glad to have you back, Agent P,"
Carl said. Then they zoomed away.

Major Monogram told Agent P that
he needed to find Dr. Doofenshmirtz.
The evil doctor was planning a new
scheme. And he was on the same
island as Phineas and Ferb!

The platypus climbed onto a jet
shaped like an ice-cream cone.
He flew to the desert island.

When he reached the island,
Agent P landed inside a volcano.
"Ahh! Perry the Platypus!"
Dr. Doofenshmirtz shouted.

Dr. Doofenshmirtz used a film to
explain his evil plan to Agent P.

"I am planning to provide the entire
Tri-State Area with free laundry!"
he cried.

If he did everyone's laundry for free, all the laundromats in the Tri-State Area would shut down. Dr. Doofenshmirtz planned to use the empty buildings to start his own schools of evil. Then he would have lots of students to help him with his schemes!

"I'm here on this deserted island because I get all this free monkey labor!" Dr. Doofenshmirtz explained. "I control them all!" He laughed.

Meanwhile, on the other side of
the island, Candace saw Phineas and
Ferb's tree house. It was huge!

"Can't you just be normal for one
day?" she yelled. "All you had to do
was make a little lean-to!"

"There's survival, and then there's living!" exclaimed Phineas. "Let us give you a quick tour."

In the family room, there was a
hammock and a cozy fire.

In the kitchen, monkeys baked pies.

In the bathroom, Ferb was giving
a monkey a shower.

"Had to be done," he said.

Back inside the volcano, Agent P
was fighting with Dr. Doofenshmirtz.

The doctor fell into the washing machine! The monkeys threw laundry and soap into the machine.

"What are you doing?" Dr. Doofenshmirtz shouted.

The monkeys poured in extra suds.

Then they pressed the "start" button.

The washing machine spun and shook.

Soapsuds bubbled out and over
the top!

The monkeys screeched and ran away.

Agent P jumped onto an ironing board. He used it to surf away from the volcano.

On the other side of the island,
Isabella saw the suds and
thought they were lava.

"Volcano!" she yelled to Phineas and
Ferb. "We need to move now!"

The friends made it out of the tree
house just in time.

They quickly found Candace.

"Run!" warned Phineas. "Pink lava behind you!"

Near the shore, Phineas and Ferb's
parents finished fixing the boat.
But it was still stuck.

The kids ran up. The pink soapsuds were right behind them!

"We've got to get out of here!" cried Candace.

They all climbed the ladder to
the boat.

The wave of soapsuds pushed
the boat off the rock.

No one noticed that Agent P caught
a ride on the back of the boat.

Back at Phineas and Ferb's house,
Baljeet thought Perry was missing.
He used a baseball cap and a frozen
waffle to make a fake Perry.

But he was pretty sure Phineas and
Ferb would know the difference.

"We have to tell them the truth!"
Baljeet cried.

Soon Phineas and Ferb arrived home. "Wait until you hear what we did," Phineas said.

"I have something to tell you," Baljeet said sadly.

Just then, Perry walked by. Baljeet couldn't believe his eyes!

"Thanks, Baljeet," Phineas said. "I knew we could count on you."

Perry Speaks!

Adapted by **Ellie O'Ryan**

Based on the series created by
Dan Povenmire & Jeff "Swampy" Marsh

One summer day, Phineas and Ferb were in the backyard with Perry.

"What to do today," Phineas said. "Any ideas, Ferb?"

Ferb just shrugged.

"How about you, Perry?" Phineas asked.

Perry made his chittering noise.

"I wonder what that means," Phineas said. "Let's build a Perry translator!"

The boys went right to work.
"Now we need our subject,"
said Phineas. "Where's Perry?"

The brothers looked left and right. They looked up and down. Perry had disappeared!

Perry put on his hat to transform
into Agent P. Then he used a remote
control to enter his hidden lair.

He had a meeting with
Major Monogram!

"We're saving paper by printing on the same piece over and over again," Major Monogram said. "I can't make this out. Well, I'm sure it says something about Doofenshmirtz. Go get him!"

Agent P ran through the backyard.
"Oh, there you are!" Phineas said.
"It's time to hear what's on your
mind."

Just then, Isabella came into the yard. "What'cha doin'?" she asked.

"We invented a Perry translator," Phineas replied.

"Great!" Isabella said. "But don't you need Perry?"

Phineas turned around. Perry had disappeared again!

Just then, the friends heard a
squeaky voice.

"I sure love worms!" it said. "Big,
juicy worms! Got to find them."

A bird had landed on the translator's microphone.

The invention really worked!

"With a device like this, animals can finally say what's on their minds!" Phineas said.

The bird overheard Phineas. It went to tell some pigeons.

The pigeons told a dog.

The dog told a bunch of cats.
Soon all the animals in Danville
were on their way to Phineas and
Ferb's backyard!

A chubby orange cat meowed.
It wanted more food.

"They're giving you twelve cans
a day," Phineas said. "Technically,
you're not underfed."

Next a black dog barked.

"I've been hearing a lot about the vacuum," Phineas replied.

Meanwhile, across town, Agent P found Dr. Doofenshmirtz deep in the forest. The platypus was about to sneak up on him when . . .

Thwack!

A giant cage landed on Agent P.

Dr. Doofenshmirtz told the platypus his evil plan.

"With this remote, I will open the Danville Dam, flooding the streets," he said.

"People will have to buy my latest invention to get around. It's like a car, but it can drive on water."

He yanked a sheet off a large boat. "I call it the Buoyancy Operated Aquatic Transport, or BO-AT, for short," he said. "Everyone will want one!"

Back at home,
Candace's phone
beeped. It was
Jeremy! He asked
if she wanted to
play video games.

Knock-
knock-
knock!

"Hold on. Someone's at the door,"
Jeremy said.

It was Candace! She had run all the
way from her house.

"So, video games?" she asked.

Candace and Jeremy started playing a game. Suddenly, a poodle jumped up on the couch.

The dog growled at Candace.

Then it peed on her shoe!

Candace tried to dry her shoe
with paper towels. But the dog ran
off with it!

Candace chased the dog into the
bathroom. It held her shoe over the
toilet.

"Don't even think about it!" Candace
warned.

Candace tried to flush the paper
towels down the toilet. Then the
dog dropped the shoe in. The toilet
clogged up!

"No!" Candace cried. Paper towels and toilet water exploded all over the bathroom.

Candace ran home.

Meanwhile, in the backyard, Isabella gave Phineas an update.

"We've got seventy-eight complaints about food," she said. "And forty-two requests for belly rubs."

One of the Fireside Girls joined them. "This hamster says it's going to lose it if someone doesn't oil the wheel in its cage," she said.

"Let's tell the owners what their pets want!" Phineas exclaimed.

Just then, Candace got home.

"I have had it with stupid animals today!" she shouted.

The animals didn't like that.

A big dog barked.

"Get her!" the machine translated.

In the forest, Dr. Doofenshmirtz
opened the Danville Dam.

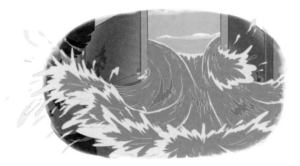

Water flooded out.

Luckily, the water knocked over
Agent P's cage. The platypus swam to
the BO-AT and jumped on.

Across town, the animals chased
Candace through the city . . .

. . . and into the forest!

Suddenly, the water freed from the
dam washed over everything. It swept
the animals up into the BO-AT!

The water rushed toward downtown Danville. Agent P swam as fast as he could to a high wall with a wheel on it.

"Don't open that!" the doctor cried.

Agent P turned the wheel.
A moat around Danville opened. All
the water flowed around the city.
Danville was saved!

Perry sneaked back home. When Phineas, Ferb, and Isabella returned to the yard, Perry was waiting for them.

Candace hurried home, too. She
dragged her mom into the backyard.
   "Mom, you've got to see this!"
she cried.

"Okay," Phineas said. "We've been waiting all day for this."

Perry made his chittering noise. Everyone waited. Then . . .

Brbrbrbrbrbrbr!

The animal translator played the chittering noise right back!

"Oh, well," Phineas said. "I guess it doesn't mean anything."

Just then, Jeremy walked up. "Hey, Candace!" he called. "I brought your shoe. I washed it. Here, allow me."

Jeremy slipped the shoe onto Candace's foot. She felt just like a princess—and fainted!

"Candace? You okay?" Jeremy asked.

"Enchanted!" she replied.

Attack of the Ferb Snatchers!

Adapted by **Kristen Depken**

Based on the series created by
Dan Povenmire & Jeff "Swampy" Marsh

Late one night, Phineas and Ferb
were watching alien movies. Candace
decided to watch, too.

"Get me up to speed," she said.

"There are three classic ways to spot an alien," said Phineas.

Aliens used strange words.

Aliens had weird body parts.

"But the clearest sign," said Phineas, "is that they can remove any human head and replace it with their own head."

The alien movie played all night.

In the end, no one thought the woman in the movie had really seen aliens. "Why did I think anyone would believe me?" she cried. "I was a fool!"

"That was awesome!" Candace said.

She looked around.

Phineas and Ferb were gone.

Candace ran to find her brothers. She bumped into her mom, who was carrying a basket of laundry.

The basket fell on the floor.

"Can you take this upstairs?" her mom asked.

Candace held up one of Ferb's shirts. "Cute," she said. "Ferb's torso is so tiny."

Candace found Ferb upstairs. He was talking to someone on the computer.

But Ferb's words sounded strange.

Candace left. She didn't see Ferb take a piece of candy out of his mouth. Ferb hadn't been talking at all. The voice Candace heard was Ferb's cousin. He had a Scottish accent.

Later, Ferb went to the backyard.
He began working on a project.
Candace saw Ferb's shadow
through a tent. It looked like
Ferb was taking off his head!

"Ferb's an alien!" Candace yelled.
She hid in the basement.

Then Candace ran to tell Phineas. "Ferb is an alien!" she said.

"I think you might be letting your imagination get the best of you," Phineas replied.

Candace decided to get proof!
She spied on Ferb and took pictures.

Meanwhile, Perry was on a mission. The platypus needed to stop Dr. Doofenshmirtz from selling evil inventions on the Internet.

Agent P dressed up like a mad scientist. Then he went to the doctor's lab.

"You must be here about the ad," Dr. Doofenshmirtz said.

The doctor took Agent P over to a big machine. "Behold: the Wrapped Up in a Nice Little Bow-inator!" he said. "Tidying up is a snap with a press of this button."

The doctor pushed the button.

The machine zapped a pile of dirty sheets on Dr. Doofenshmirtz's bed.

The bed shrunk into a tiny box!

"You can also use the machine
to hang your clothes on. Just like
a treadmill," he said.

Just then, Agent P pulled off his disguise! Dr. Doofenshmirtz grabbed a baseball bat.

Agent P used his tail to whack the tiny box with the bow at the doctor.

The box hit the treadmill's "start" button.

The treadmill began to move! Dr. Doofenshmirtz accidentally knocked over his baseball collection.

Baseballs bounced everywhere!
They hit the red button on the
Wrapped Up in a Nice Little
Bow-inator.

Soon everything in the lab was
shrinking into tiny boxes.

Back at home, Candace showed
Phineas the pictures she had taken.
"Ferb is an alien!" she cried.

Phineas took Candace outside.
Ferb was working in his tent.

"I saw Ferb's head ripped off by an
alien monster!" Candace insisted.

"Oh, you must mean this reverse
power unit," Phineas explained.

He pulled back the tent flap.

Inside was a machine that was shaped
like Ferb's head.

"But what about all this evidence?" Candace asked.

"We're fixing a spacecraft for a friend," Phineas explained.

"Wait, what?" Candace said.

"We just finished, and it's about to launch," Phineas replied.

Candace couldn't believe it. "You guys are so busted!" she shouted.

Candace ran to get her mother.
"Mom, I've got something to show
you!" she exclaimed.

Candace dragged her mother to
the backyard.

Suddenly, the lawn opened up.
A giant spaceship and launching pad
rose out of the ground.

"I can't believe this is really happening!" Candace said to her brothers. "I busted you!"

But their mom just smiled. "You two have done a great job repairing my ship," she said.

"Huh?" asked Candace.

The "mom" in the yard was really
a robot. Inside was a tiny alien!

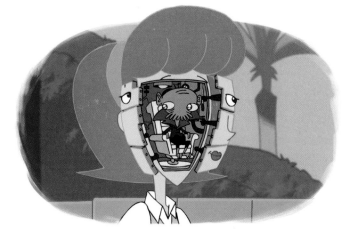

"No problem, Garr-bagg!" Phineas
said. The brothers had fixed the
alien's broken spaceship.

Candace was shocked. There had
been an alien. And her brothers had
gotten away with helping it!

Their real mom's car pulled
into the driveway. The alien ship
and robot mom were gone, but the
launchpad was still in the backyard.

"I have proof!" cried Candace.
She ran to get her real mom.

Back at Dr. Doofenshmirtz's lab,
Agent P hit a tiny box at his enemy.

The doctor accidentally swallowed
it. His stomach began to rumble.

The furniture in the box expanded!

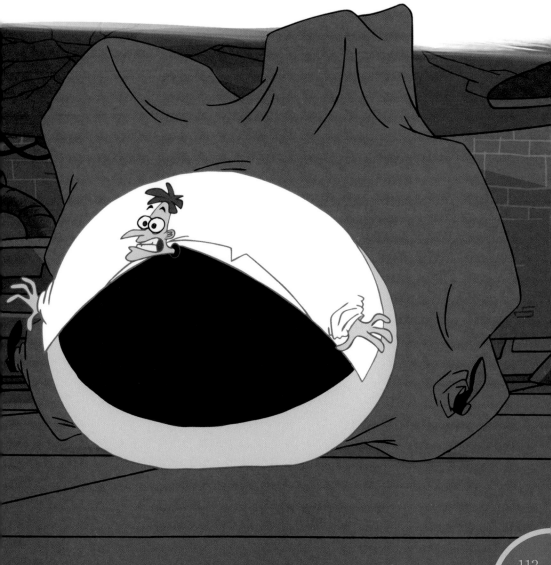

Suddenly, the Wrapped Up in a Nice Little Bow-inator rolled out the window. Agent P jumped on the machine and pressed the button.

Dr. Doofenshmirtz's whole lab shrank into a tiny box with a bow.

Agent P flew away on a parachute.

Before it hit the ground, the machine shot one last laser beam up into the air. It bounced off a satellite . . .

. . . and right into Phineas and
Ferb's backyard! The alien launchpad
shrunk into a tiny box.

A moment later, Candace brought
her mom into the backyard. By that
point, the launchpad was gone.

"No!" cried Candace. "But it was all
right here."

Candace dropped to her knees.

"Oh, why did I think anyone would believe me?" she cried. "I was a fool! A fool!"

Candace's life suddenly seemed a lot like a movie.

Boogie Down

Adapted by **Kristen Depken**

Based on the series created by
Dan Povenmire & Jeff "Swampy" Marsh

It was a special day in Danville.
The television show *Let's All Dance
Until We're Sick* was in town.
They were looking for new dancers.

"I've already entered us!" Candace
told Jeremy.

"I'm going to get some fresh air,"
Jeremy said.

Jeremy went to the backyard.
Phineas and Ferb were there.

Jeremy said he was worried about
the show.

He didn't think he was a good
dancer.

"Maybe Ferb can teach you!"
Phineas said.

Ferb wiggled
his arms.

He kicked his legs.

He jumped
and did a split.

"There's no way I can learn that by tonight," Jeremy said.

"Maybe you don't have to," Phineas replied. "Ferb, I know what we're going to do today!"

Then Phineas looked around the yard. "Hey, where's Perry?"

Agent P was in his lair. He had another mission.

Major Monogram told him the plan.
Dr. Doofenshmirtz had bought all the
potatoes, bacon, and green onions in
the Tri-State Area.

"It sounds like a recipe for evil,"
Major Monogram said. "So get
cooking, Agent P!"

Agent P zoomed off
to Dr. Doofenshmirtz's
headquarters. But
when he got there, he
was caught in a trap!

"Well, well, well." The doctor
laughed. "All shackled up and no
place to go."

The doctor and his robot used all
the potatoes, bacon, and onions to
make a big bucket of potato salad.

"I'm off to our annual evil potluck,"
he said. He aimed a laser at the
platypus. "I'll just leave you here
to meet your doom."

Dr. Doofenshmirtz left.

The laser beam moved toward
Agent P.

Fortunately, Dr. Doofenshmirtz
wasn't good at making traps.

Agent P easily slipped out of the
cuffs.

Back at home, Phineas and Ferb
built a machine called the
Ferbulistic Groove-a-Tron 9000.

"You wear it under your clothes,"
Phineas explained.

If Jeremy wore it, he could copy
any dance move Ferb did.

Ferb raised his arms. So did Jeremy.

Ferb did a disco pose. Jeremy did, too!

"Sweet!" Jeremy exclaimed.

Meanwhile, Dr. Doofenshmirtz met up with some other scientists. They were members of an evil club.

Dr. Doofenshmirtz had invited all the reporters in town to the meeting. He wanted everyone to know about the club's evil plans.

But the reporters were all at the
dance contest.

"To the dance hall!" the doctor
exclaimed.

The contest had already started.
"Attention, citizens of Danville!"
Dr. Doofenshmirtz yelled.

But no one paid attention.

The cameras were all on the best
dancers.

"Split up and start dancing like
you've never danced before," the
doctor told his friends. "Whoever
gets on camera first can deliver our
evil message."

A scientist named Rodney thought he could dance better than everyone else. "This looks like a job for—" he started.

"Can it, Rodney!" Dr. Doofenshmirtz snapped. "I'm a better dancer than you."

Just then, Agent P arrived at the contest. Major Monogram sent him a message.

"You must stop Doofenshmirtz and his group before they broadcast their evil message and interrupt what has quickly become my favorite show," Major Monogram ordered.

Backstage, it was time to put the Ferbulistic Groove-a-Tron 9000 to the test!

Ferb wiggled his arms. He shrugged his shoulders. He got groovy.

The machine helped Jeremy do the same moves.

Dr. Doofenshmirtz tried to get on camera. He danced as hard as he could.

"You may begin quaking in fear," he said into the camera.

BZZZZ!

His spotlight went out. The doctor was eliminated.

Rodney tried, too. "Hello, future subjects," he said.

BZZZ!

His spotlight went out.

Across the stage, Jeremy's dancing
was amazing, thanks to Ferb.

Candace's friend Stacy threw a
bouquet of flowers.

A bee flew out of the flowers.
It buzzed over to Ferb! He swatted
at the bee.

Because of the machine, Jeremy started swatting the air. Everyone thought it was a new dance move.

Dr. Doofenshmirtz and Rodney started pushing dancers out of their spotlights.

"If anyone's pushing this dancer out of the way, it's me!" the doctor yelled.

"I was here first!" Rodney shouted back.

They battled over the spotlight.
It looked like they were dancing!
Dr. Doofenshmirtz sighed.
"This is awkward," he said.

Just then, Agent P soared above the dance floor.

Wham! He knocked into a disco ball.

The disco ball crashed right on top
of Rodney and Dr. Doofenshmirtz!
Agent P's mission was a success.

The thud from the disco ball knocked Jeremy to center stage. He was the only dancer left.

With the machine's help, Jeremy danced so quickly that his feet became a blur. He ended in a split. The crowd went wild!

"How would you like to dance until you're sick every week?" the contest host asked Jeremy.

"Do it!" Candace cried.

Jeremy shook his head. He pulled the Ferbulistic Groove-a-Tron 9000 out of his clothes. "This was doing all those dance moves," he explained.

Then Jeremy pulled the curtain back to reveal Ferb.

"It looks like my work here is done," Ferb said.

He danced offstage.

The judges gave Ferb a perfect score.

"I'm sorry, Candace," Jeremy said.
"I didn't want to let you down."

"I just wanted us to have fun," Candace said. "You know, dance until we're sick."

"Well, I am feeling a little dizzy," Jeremy replied.

"I've got you," Candace said.

With Phineas and Ferb's help, Jeremy had really boogied down.

And he was pretty sure that he had done enough dancing to last him a lifetime!